JAMES AND THE DIESEL ENGINES

by

Christopher Awdry

with illustrations by
Clive Spong

LITTLE
MAMMOTH

Crossed Lines

MOST of the Fat Controller's engines accepted diesels. James had never liked them.

"They're all right," said Henry. "Just mixed-traffic engines like you and me."

"Mixed-up engines, you mean," James grunted. "With windows at each end how can they know if they're coming or going?"

"Toby has two cabs," remarked Duck, "and he gets on all right."

"Toby's just a little engine," scoffed James. "If an important engine like me didn't know which way to turn, what would the Railway come to?"

All the engines agreed that James was becoming much too puffed up in his smoke-box.

"Making out he's Royalty or something," grumbled Henry. "It's disgusting."

"I knew an engine called King James," remarked Duck. "In the old days, at Paddington. King James I he was, but he didn't swank about like that."

"Och, dinna be telling James that," pleaded Donald. "It's even mair of a misery he'll be makkin' oor lives."

"Exactly," agreed Henry, "but who's going to trim his wheels for him?"

The engines tried all sorts of ideas, but nothing worked. James grew so conceited that the others were glad when he was away. Even the coaches twittered anxiously to each other if they thought he was to pull them.

One day James came to the shed, fuming with rage.

"Shunting!" he snorted. "Where are Donald and Douglas? They should be here for jobs like that."

But the Twins were helping on Edward's branch line, so James had to do the work himself.

James's train had long trucks called well-wagons. These have bogie-wheels at each end, with a low section between them. They are used to carry cars, tractors and other heavy machinery.

The shunting should have been easy, but James was cross and bumped the trucks.

"Oh, oh, oh, oh, oh!" they cried. Some of them slipped their brakes "on" to spite James. The weather was damp and misty too, so the shunting took a long time.

At last James had only two trucks to fetch before his train was ready.

Because of the mist, the signalman sometimes found it hard to see what was happening. James's driver told him that James would whistle when they had collected all the trucks and were clear of the points. They had almost finished when suddenly James heard a sharp "Peep peep" from another engine close by.

The signalman heard it too, and thought it was James saying he was ready. He pulled the lever, setting the points for the main line.

But James wasn't ready. The points changed when one of the trucks was half-way over them; one bogie went the right way, but the other was diverted towards the main line. Before James realised it, the truck was travelling sideways between the two lines. A signal stood right in its path.

"Stop!" squealed the truck, but it was too late. The signal toppled to the ground with a crash, just missing James.

"That's torn it!" said James's driver. "The Fat Controller won't like that."

He didn't. He spoke severely about it, because the signal was important and its loss was inconvenient.

James knew that the accident was not his fault, but he was unusually quiet in the shed that evening. The others were relieved.

"I suppose it *must* be difficult to know which way to go when you've got two cabs," whispered a voice, "but to go two ways at once with only one cab—that really is something!"

James pretended he hadn't heard.

Deep Freeze

WINTER had come, and for many days now had held everything in an icy grip. The countryside was frozen hard, trees were white with frost, and icicles hung from bridges and water-columns. Mercifully there was little snow.

"Too cold for that, thank goodness," shivered James's driver, as he and the fireman huddled on the sheltered side of the cab. James had an open footplate, and every day his crew came to work muffled to the eyebrows in scarves and jerseys.

Sometimes water-columns froze too, and then the engines could not get the water they needed. But this never happened at the Works station, and one day, when the frost seemed harder than ever, James's driver stopped him beside the water-column there.

"We'll give you a good topping-up while we can," he said. "There's no telling when we might get some more."

James shivered as the icy water cascaded into his tender, but he knew his driver was right.

They filled James's tank to the brim, because the fireman forgot to tell the driver to turn the tap off. Water overflowed onto James's tender, making him shiver again.

"Right," said the fireman, jumping down to the footplate. "Let's be off—I want to warm myself up shovelling coal."

"We can't go yet," laughed the driver. "They haven't finished loading the luggage van."

"Well I wish they'd hurry," grumbled the fireman, blowing on his hands. "I'm frozen from standing on that tender."

All engines have a tap called an injector. It allows the driver or fireman to transfer water from the tender to the boiler, and is very important. Without it the water-level in the boiler could become too low to make steam properly.

They had not gone far before James felt thirsty.

"I need a drink, please," he said.

His driver switched on the injector but nothing happened. The fireman tried his duplicate; still nothing.

"I've got such a pain," groaned James.

"Your injector's failed," said his driver. "Blockage in the pipe most likely. We'll have to stop and deal with your fire—can't go on without water."

"Don't set the sleepers on fire," pleaded James. "Henry would never let me forget it."

The fireman laughed.

"You'll be all right if we just damp you down," he said. "There's no need to throw the fire out, as Henry did."

They stopped near a signal-box and James's driver asked the signalman to telephone for help.

The Works sent a diesel, whom James had never met, to help him.

"Rescued by a diesel," he snorted disgustedly. "It's degrading. I won't go!"

But he soon changed his mind, because now that his fire was down his boiler was cooling and he could feel the icy wind.

The diesel was friendly. James was quiet at first, but by the time they reached the works the diesel had won him over and the two of them were chatting like old friends.

At the Works, James's fireman climbed on to the tender. He tried to open the filler-cap but couldn't.

"There's your answer, James," he said. "Your filler-cap's frozen solid. That's because the water overflowed. Ice is stopping air from getting into the tank, so the injectors can't work. You'll be all right when the ice melts."

He was, and that wasn't all. Thanks to his new friend from the Works, even James now admits that diesels can be useful engines too.

The stories in *James and the Diesel Engines* first appeared in
James and the Diesel Engines, Railway Series No. 28
First published in Great Britain 1984
This edition published 1992 by Little Mammoth
an imprint of Mandarin Paperbacks
Michelin House, 81 Fulham Road, London SW3 6RB

Mandarin is an imprint of the Octopus Publishing Group

Text and illustrations copyright © William Heinemann Ltd 1992

ISBN 0 7497 0883 2

A CIP catalogue record for this title
is available from the British Library

Reproduced from original artwork
by Dot Gradations Ltd, Chelmsford, Essex

Typeset by Rowland Phototypesetting Ltd
Bury St Edmunds, Suffolk

Printed in Great Britain
by Scotprint Ltd, Musselburgh, Scotland

Little Mammoth Railway Series